The Adventure of the Buried Treasure

by Nancy McArthur

Illustrated by

Irene Trivas

A
LITTLE APPLE
PAPERBACK

SCHOLASTIC INC.

New York Toronto London Auckland Sydney

ISBN 0-590-43466-7

12 11 10 9 8   5/9

Printed in the U.S.A.   **40**

First Scholastic printing, September 1990

Other books by Nancy McArthur

Pickled Peppers
Megan Gets a Dollhouse

Chapter 1

Puddles walked around his backyard sniffing everywhere. He could tell by his nose who had been here.

He smelled the squirrels and the big orange cat from next door. That cat better not come over when Pud was outside!

All over he smelled the rabbits that hopped around at night. He also smelled his people. They walked on only two feet.

Susie was his main person. She gave him food and water and hugged him. He slept next to her bed at night.

Susie's mom and dad were his other people. They did what Pud wanted most of the time. But Mom made loud noises when he dug in the yard or came in with muddy feet.

Pud stopped. A dog he'd never smelled before had been here. He also smelled a bone. A strange dog had buried a bone in his yard!

He started digging fast. If Mom saw him, she would make loud noises.

Mom looked out the window. "Pud's digging up the yard!" she screeched.

Susie sighed. Pud was her dog, so she had to stop him. She and her friend Annie were busy watching Saturday morning cartoons. Maybe Pud would stop before Mom screeched again.

"Get out there and stop him!" screamed Mom. Susie slid off the couch. She hurried through the kitchen and out the back door. "Pud, stop that!" she yelled.

Pud had just got at the bone. His claws scraped on something hard underneath it. He saw Mom in the window waving her arms. She was making very loud noises.

"Ugh," said Susie. "What do you want with that yucky old bone?" Pud took it in his teeth and walked away. Susie got down on her knees next to the hole to put the dirt back.

She saw the corner of something rusty. What could it be? She needed something to dig with.

Mom called out the back door, "I'm going across the street to the Smiths'. I'll be right back."

Susie went in the house. "I found something buried in the backyard," she told Annie. "Want to help me dig it up?"

3

"Sure," said Annie.

Susie got two big spoons from the kitchen. "It might be a buried treasure," she said.

"Yards don't have buried treasures," said Annie.

"I'm digging it up anyway," said Susie.

Pud sat in a corner of the yard watching the girls. They didn't know how to dig. They were using long things instead of their paws.

The ground was hard. "These spoons aren't sharp enough," complained Annie.

Next door the big orange cat jumped up on the kitchen table to look out the window. Something interesting was going on.

"Fluffo," said Megan, "get off the table before Mom sees you!" Fluffo paid no attention. So Megan looked out the window, too.

"They're digging!" she said. "I'm going over there." Fluffo jumped down to follow. She scratched behind his ears. "You have to stay in. Susie's dog is out there." She opened the door just enough to squeeze through, with no room for Fluffo. He clawed at the closed door. Then he jumped back on the table to watch.

"What's going on?" Megan asked Susie.

"This might be a buried treasure," Susie said. "I'm going to look in the garage for something better to dig with."

"I'll help you look," said Megan. "Annie, you guard the treasure until we get back."

Annie giggled. "I'll get Pud to help me keep robbers and space monsters away." They all giggled.

Susie and Megan came back with a shovel

and a hoe. They all took turns chopping at the dirt. It was still too hard.

"I wish this were mud," said Susie.

"We can make it into mud," said Megan. She turned on the hose and dragged it over to the hole.

"How long does it take?" asked Annie.

"I don't know," said Megan. They sat down to wait.

"What do you think the treasure will be?" asked Megan.

"Money," said Annie.

"Maybe gold and jewels," said Susie. She giggled. "Or pizza!"

"Or chocolate chip cookies!" said Annie.

"Very old chocolate chip cookies!" added Megan.

"Very moldy chocolate chip cookies!" shouted Susie.

"Oldie moldy chocolate chip pizza!" yelled Megan. "With green slime!" They rolled around on the grass, laughing.

"Yuck," said Susie. Her sleeve was all wet. The hose had made a big puddle. "Do you think it's mud enough yet?" she asked.

They chopped at the muddy ground. "The water takes a long time to soak down," said Megan, "but it's getting easier." They kept chopping.

Pud got tired of watching the girls. He saw something more interesting — the big orange cat. He would show that cat whose yard this was! He ran over and growled under the window.

Chapter 2

Finally the girls got the top of the rusty thing uncovered. It was about as big as the top of a lunch box.

"If it's a treasure," said Megan, "it's not a big one."

"My grandma always says good things come in small packages," said Annie. "Every time she gives me a small package."

Eric came around the side of the house with his baseball and mitt. "Have you seen Tim?" he asked. "We're supposed to play catch."

Megan sat down on the hole in case they didn't want Eric to see what was in it.

"Why are you sitting on that hole?" he asked.

"We can tell him," said Susie. "Cross your heart and promise not to tell?" she asked.

"Sure, what is it?"

Megan stood up.

"That's just a rusty old can," said Eric.

Megan was disgusted. For trying to keep the treasure secret, she'd just gotten mud all over her pants. "You don't know anything," she said. "It's a buried treasure."

"Like from pirates?" asked Eric.

"Maybe," said Susie. "We have to dig it up to find out."

"But," said Annie, "pirates always sail the seas. We don't have any seas around here, so pirates couldn't come to this yard."

Susie started digging again. "Maybe there were seas here a million years ago."

"I want to dig, too," said Eric. He put his

ball and mitt down far from the mud. Megan handed him a spoon.

"But," said Annie, "a million years ago, there weren't any pirates, just dinosaurs."

Susie laughed. "Maybe a dinosaur did this."

They all chopped at the ground. With the water running into the hole, it was getting muddier.

The rusty thing finally came loose. Susie pulled it out. The lid was rusted shut.

"It looks like a lunch box," said Megan, "but really old."

"We dug up somebody's old lunch?" asked Eric.

"Why would somebody bury a lunch?" asked Annie.

"Maybe it was something they really hated," said Susie, "like a pickle and onion sandwich."

She shook the box. It rattled like a piggy bank!

Pud got tired of bothering the cat. Now he was snoozing on an old rug in the garage. He opened his eyes to see what the new rattling noise was. Even though they did not know how to dig, they had dug up something. And it wasn't a bone. His nose told him that from all the way over here. Mom was making loud noises again, but not at him. He went back to sleep.

Mom zoomed out the back door. "What are you doing?" she shouted. "I sent you out here to stop the dog from digging. Now I come back, and *you're* digging! My spoons! They're all bent!"

"We can bend them back," said Susie. "See, Pud found a buried treasure! It sounds like money, but we can't get it open."

"I know Pud didn't dig this big a hole," said Mom. "Not unless he just learned how to use a shovel and spoons."

"He did too find it when he dug up a bone," explained Susie. "A little corner of the box was sticking out. So we had to dig it up."

"It's an old lunch box," said Mom. "It looks like it's been in the ground a long time. Some kid must have put it here."

"I hope it was a rich kid," said Eric.

Mom told Susie, "Go get me a screwdriver and a hammer. I will try to get this open. The rest of you fill this hole up. What a mess!"

They had a good time smearing the mud back into the hole. Then Mom made them wash their hands with the hose. They squirted water at each other and laughed. Then they gathered around to watch.

Mom put the point of the screwdriver

under the lid's edge. She whacked the screwdriver handle with the hammer.

Pud yawned and looked out of the garage. Now they were making new noises with what they dug up. It wasn't even something they could chew on. People did strange things.

Chapter 3

After a lot of banging, the lid came loose. "Let me open it," said Susie. She bent the rusty hinges a little and peeked in. "Oh!" she said.

Annie, Eric, and Megan bumped heads with Susie trying to look in. Annie's elbow stuck Megan in the ribs. Eric stepped on Annie's foot.

"Stand back," said Mom, "so we can all see."

Susie pulled the lid all the way open. Inside they saw two dimes, two nickels, five pennies, a green eraser, a yellow pencil, and a folded paper.

"That's not a treasure," said Eric.

"Well, it's money," said Megan.

"Not much," said Annie.

"All together thirty-five cents," said Mom.

Susie unfolded the paper carefully. It was wrapped around a baseball card. "This is a message!" she said.

"From the pirates or the dinosaurs?" joked Eric.

"It's from Eddie," she replied.

"Eddie who?" asked Megan.

"I don't know." Susie read the message to herself first. Then she passed it around. It read:

DEAR Who FiNDS this iN 100 YEArs,
I GOT A NEW LunchboX So I MADE
this ONE A TiME CAPSOOL.
YOU CAN SPEND THE MONEY
AND USE MY PENCiL. YOU CAN
KEEP the bAseBall CArd. I
hAVE ANOTHER ONE jUST LiKE
it. I AM iN SECOND GrADE
At ELM PARK SchooL. GOOD LucK.
                    YOUR FiEND,
                    EDDIE
P.S. I hoPE MY DOG WON'T
     DiG this UP beFORE YoU
     FiND it.

"This is from a fiend," said Annie, looking worried, "and he goes to our school."

"No," said Eric. "He means *friend*, only he left out the R. I spell friend 'fiend' sometimes when I'm in a hurry."

"That's why we have erasers," said Mom. "Everybody makes mistakes. I'm going in to fix lunch. Don't put your hands in your mouths after you touched all that old stuff. Wait till you get home, and wash with soap and hot water."

Pud heard the word "lunch." He got up and stretched. Then he jogged over to the back door and woofed. Mom let him in.

"Eddie shouldn't have buried his eraser," said Eric. "I need mine all the time."

"Me, too," said Susie. "Maybe he got a

new one." The eraser felt hard as a rock. She passed it around.

Megan said, "This must be really old. It feels like an eraser fossil."

Eric picked up the baseball card. "Joe DiMaggio," he read. "That's a great player. This card looks old. Maybe it's worth some money."

"How much do baseball cards cost?" asked Annie.

"I have some that cost me a few cents apiece," replied Eric. "But once I paid two dollars for a really good one."

"Wow," said Annie.

"Is this a two-dollar one?" asked Susie.

"I can find out," said Eric.

Pud was already under the table when his people sat down for lunch. He waited with his head on his paws, watching their shoes and socks. Then Susie's fingers came down with a little piece of meat. He could always depend on Susie.

Susie told Dad all about the treasure. "Why did Eddie bury his lunch box here?" she wondered. "Why didn't he do it in his own yard?"

"Maybe," said Dad, "a long time ago, this *was* his yard."

"That can't be," said Susie. "We have always lived here."

"We've lived here all *your* life," said Dad. "That's seven years. Before you were born, your mother and I lived in an apartment. We bought this house from the Kirk family."

Susie was amazed. She'd never thought that somebody else might have lived in their house. "Did they have an Eddie?" she asked.

"No," said Mom. "They had all girls."

"The Kirks lived here about fifteen years," said Dad. "Our seven years and their fifteen add up to twenty-two. So Eddie must have lived here more than twenty-two years ago."

"Wow," said Susie. "Then he doesn't go to our school anymore."

Chapter 4

Eric met Tim on his way home and told him the news. "Let's get your mitt and play catch," said Eric.

"First I want to see what you dug up," said Tim. He headed for Susie's house. Eric followed.

Susie showed Tim the lunch box. "Only thirty-five cents?" he said. "That's not a treasure!"

"Is too," said Eric. "That money is really old."

"How old?"

"Twenty-two," said Susie. "Maybe older."

"Wow," said Tim.

Susie showed him the message from Eddie. "Don't touch it," she said. "You might tear it."

"No, I won't," he said. He grabbed one corner. It tore right off.

Susie lost her temper. "I told you not to touch it! Now you wrecked it!"

Tim looked really sorry. "I can go home and get some tape to fix it," he said.

He looked so sorry that Susie felt bad about yelling at him. "We have tape," she said. "It's just the corner, not the writing part."

Tim looked at the baseball card, but did not pick it up. "Do you want to sell this?" he asked. "I'll give you ten cents."

"No, but I might want to later if it's a two-dollar one."

"That's too much," said Tim. He wanted

to see where they dug up the lunch box.

"That's just a bunch of mud," Tim said, "not a hole."

"It used to be a hole," Susie said. "My mom made us fill it up."

"Where did you get the mud?"

"They made it with the hose," said Eric.

"Let's go over to my house and make mud," said Tim.

"What for?" asked Eric.

"Mud balls," replied Tim.

Eric laughed. "I'm not playing catch with those!" he said.

After Tim and Eric left, Susie went to the living room to talk to Mom. "Eddie doesn't go to our school anymore, so how am I going to find him?"

"Why do you want to?" asked Mom.

"To tell him I found his stuff. He wanted somebody to dig it up. I can write him a letter."

Mom replied, "That was a long time ago. Maybe he wouldn't even remember that he buried that old lunch box."

"I want to find him anyway," said Susie, "but I don't know how."

"You and your friends could go around the neighborhood and ask questions."

"Like detectives!" exclaimed Susie. "What do we ask?"

"Find out who's lived around here the longest. Maybe someone remembers a family who lived here that had an Eddie."

"I'll go next door and ask Mrs. Johnson first. She knows everybody."

"Take Pud with you," said Mom. "He needs a walk."

Pud heard the word "walk." He galloped to the door and wagged his tail. To get Susie to hurry, he nuzzled her knees with his nose.

She clipped the leash to his collar and opened the door.

There in his front yard was the big orange cat!

Pud sprang out the door, dragging Susie with him. The leash pulled out of her hand.

Fluffo hissed. The fur on his back stood straight up, making him look bigger. The fur on his tail puffed up.

Pud did not stop.

Fluffo turned and ran right up the nearest tree.

Pud barked and clawed at the tree trunk. He could not reach the cat. Susie grabbed his leash. She tugged and yelled. Finally Pud let Susie pull him away.

Fluffo sat high up on a branch looking down at them.

Chapter 5

Susie pulled Pud along over to Megan's and rang the bell. "Fluffo's up a tree," she told Megan. "Pud sort of chased him."

"Bad dog," scolded Megan. "You shouldn't chase my cat."

"Fluffo started it," complained Susie. "He shouldn't come in my yard. That makes Pud mad."

Megan gave Susie an angry look. Susie started to feel mad, too.

"Why don't you put your cat on a leash when he goes out?" asked Susie crossly.

"Cats are too smart to let people do that to them," snapped Megan.

"Now I'm not going to tell you what I was going to tell you!" said Susie. "I'm going over to Annie's and tell her!" She left, pulling Pud along.

"Wait up!" yelled Megan. She called to her mother that she was going over to Annie's.

First she ran over to the tree where Fluffo sat. "Come down!" she ordered. Fluffo just looked at her and blinked.

The first time Fluffo went up a tree, Megan had gotten her brother Mike to climb a ladder and rescue him. But Fluffo had clawed Mike on the way down. Then he ran in the garage and hid.

The next time Mike would not rescue Fluffo. Megan had tried but could not reach him. She thought her cat would be stuck in that tree forever. But at dinnertime, Fluffo had come to the back door. He'd gotten down by himself.

So Megan knew Fluffo was not really stuck in the tree. She hurried after Susie.

Fluffo watched Megan go down the street. His heart was still pounding from the chase. Sitting in the tree was peaceful. Leaves rustled in the breeze. He could see a long way from here.

Above him a squirrel chattered angrily. It was clinging upside down to the tree trunk, twitching its tail.

Fluffo had to sit there a while longer to show that squirrel it could not run him out of the tree. Then, when he felt like it, he would scramble down. Climbing down a tree was harder than climbing up one.

Megan caught up with Susie at Annie's house. Susie knew Megan would be good at helping to find Eddie. She decided not to be mad at her anymore.

She told her friends about other people living in her house and how they were going to be detectives. "Let's go!" said Megan.

On the way to Mrs. Johnson's they passed the tree with Fluffo in it. Pud growled.

"Don't be late for dinner," Megan called to her cat. "We're having hamburgers!" Fluffo loved hamburger.

They all liked Mrs. Johnson and her parakeet, Bitsy. Susie took care of Bitsy when Mrs. Johnson went on vacation. She was good friends with the little green bird.

Susie tied Pud's leash to a chair on Mrs. Johnson's porch.

"I'm glad to see you," Mrs. Johnson told the girls. "Come in and say hello to Bitsy. She'll be glad to see you, too."

Bitsy hopped around her cage excitedly.

"Hel-lo," said Susie.

"Hel-lo," repeated Bitsy in her funny little bird voice.

Mrs. Johnson passed around oatmeal raisin cookies. While they munched, Susie told her about Eddie and the buried treasure.

"Do you know all the people who used to live in Susie's house?" Megan asked. "Did any of them have an Eddie?"

"I remember the Kirks," replied Mrs. Johnson, "but their children were all girls."

"Who lived there before them?" asked Megan.

"I don't know. I moved here a couple of years before you were born, Susie. You were the cutest little baby!"

Susie was glad to hear about being cute, but she was disappointed that Mrs. Johnson only knew the Kirks.

"If you don't know, where are we going

to get some clues to find Eddie?" asked Susie.

"You should talk to Mrs. Amato. She's lived around here longer than anybody."

"Is that the lady with the white hair and the big brown dog?" asked Annie.

"In the yellow house around the corner?" asked Megan.

"That's her," said Mrs. Johnson.

"She's nice," said Susie. "She always waves or says hello. I didn't know her name."

Mrs. Johnson went to the phone and looked up Mrs. Amato's number. "Hello, Verna? I've got some kids here who want to talk to you. They need to know if anybody who ever lived in the white house next door to me had any boys. Good. I'll send them right over."

Megan stuck her half-eaten cookie in her pocket. Annie and Susie gobbled theirs down.

"You'd better leave Pud on my porch," said Mrs. Johnson. "If you took him along, the Amatos' dog might make a fuss."

Pud whined when the girls left him behind. Mrs. Johnson came out to give him a piece of meat and patted his head.

Chapter 6

Mrs. Amato led the girls into her sunny kitchen. She poured little glasses of orange juice for everyone. Her big brown dog ran around sniffing at all of them.

"Now what would you like to know?" asked Mrs. Amato.

Susie explained. "Do you remember all the people who used to live in my house?" she asked.

"The Kirks, and before them the Navratils, and before them the Shannons."

"Did they have any Eddies?" asked Megan.

Mrs. Amato smiled. "Only one. Eddie Shannon."

"Do you know where he moved to? We need some clues to find him," said Susie.

"I think I can find him for you," said Mrs. Amato.

"How?" asked Annie.

"Where is he?" asked Megan.

"Let me surprise you," said Mrs. Amato. "Susie, give me your phone number. I'll call you tomorrow."

Fluffo watched a long time to be sure the dog was tied up on the porch. He could walk right past that dog if he felt like it, and the dog wouldn't be able to chase him.

He scrambled down the tree trunk.

Pud saw something moving by the tree.

That cat was down on the grass right in front of Pud's house! Pud charged down the porch steps.

Mrs. Johnson's chair *ka-thumped* and bumped down the steps right behind him. He kept going, but not nearly as fast as usual.

Fluffo took off and disappeared. Pud stopped in front of his own house.

When Susie got back, there waiting for her on the lawn were Pud and the porch chair. She untied the dog. The girls dragged the chair back to Mrs. Johnson's.

"Pud sort of took your chair for a walk," explained Susie. "I hope it's not too banged up."

"If it needs fixing," said Mrs. Johnson, "you can help me."

"Mrs. Amato knows how to find Eddie," said Susie.

"Great," said Mrs. Johnson. "I'd like to meet him."

The girls hurried back to Susie's.

As they ran in, Susie shouted excitedly to Mom, "Mrs. Amato's going to find Eddie for us! His name is Eddie Shannon!"

"You're good detectives," said Mom. "Eric and Tim did detective work, too. They're here to tell you some amazing news."

The boys were in the kitchen looking at Susie's dinosaur books.

"What happened?" asked Megan.

"We went to the library!" said Eric.

"That's not amazing," said Annie. "We do that all the time."

"Let me tell," said Tim.

"No, me," said Eric. "It was my idea."

Tim said, "We got a librarian to help us look up the baseball card in a baseball card book."

"I want to tell," said Eric.

Susie asked, "Is it a two-dollar one?"

"One hundred dollars!" yelled Eric, jumping up and down. Susie had never thought about so much money in her whole life.

"Not many cards are worth a lot," said Tim, "but this one is."

Eric showed everyone a photocopy of a page from the baseball card book.

"It's a real treasure!" said Annie.

"We'll all be rich," said Eric.

"No, I'll be rich," said Susie. "My dog found the treasure in my yard."

"Then your *dog* should be rich," said Tim. "Not you."

"We all helped," said Megan.

"Yeah," said Annie. "We dug and dug and got all muddy."

"Wait a minute," said Mom. "If you find Eddie, you should give the card back. It's really his."

"He said we could have it," said Eric, "in his message."

"Finders keepers," said Susie.

Mom said, "Remember when you lost your backpack with three dollars and all your favorite stuff in it? When Annie found it, she didn't say finders keepers. She gave it back to you."

"She's my friend," said Susie. She put her arm around Annie. "Friends don't do finders keepers."

"If I kept it," said Annie, "you'd be losers weepers."

"I think Eddie is our friend," said Megan.

Susie thought so, too, but she did not want to give back the hundred-dollar baseball card. "I'll give him back his pencil and eraser," she said.

"And the thirty-five cents?" asked Eric.

"Maybe that, too," said Susie.

"What about the baseball card?" asked Annie.

Susie didn't answer. She wished everyone would forget about the baseball card.

"You need to think about this some more," said Mom. "It's time for everyone to go home now. You can all come back to-morrow."

Chapter 7

Susie had a hard time falling asleep that night.

What if Mrs. Amato couldn't find Eddie Shannon? Then Susie wouldn't have to worry. The card would be all hers, finders keepers. Maybe her friends wouldn't stay mad at her too long.

But it was Eddie's card first. He didn't know it would ever be a *real* treasure.

She sort of hoped that Eddie would not get found. But she really wanted to see him.

What would he look like? Besides, Mrs. Amato was already finding him.

Susie looked around her room in the dim light from the hall. Could this have been Eddie's room long ago? She wondered if his dog had slept next to his bed.

Susie reached down and patted Pud's fuzzy face. His legs moved a little.

Pud was dreaming about chasing the big orange cat.

The next day Annie came over right after breakfast and stayed. Eric called three times to see if Eddie was found yet. Then Tim and he came over together to wait. "Now when the phone rings," Eric said, "you'll know it isn't me."

Megan's mother wouldn't let her come over until she cleaned her room. So she cleaned very fast.

Fluffo was half snoozing in the sunshine in the kitchen. He heard Megan by the back door talking to her mother. Aha! A chance to sneak out! He yawned and waited.

Megan opened the door. A faint blur of orange fur sped past her. "Come back here!" she yelled. Fluffo disappeared into the bushes.

Megan didn't see Pud or any other dogs around. Oh, well, if one came over, Fluffo would just have to go up a tree.

At Susie's, Megan found everybody cleaning up. Susie explained, "Mom says we're going to show Eddie every room."

"Why?" asked Megan.

"Because he used to live here."

Clunking and clanking noises came from the basement. "Dad's cleaning down there," said Susie.

Mom cleaned up the kitchen. "Even if Eddie doesn't come over," she said, "at least we'll have a very clean house."

Eric and Tim helped Dad carry old junk out to the garage. Megan and Annie helped Susie clean up her room. Then Mom gave them more things to do while she ran the vacuum cleaner.

Pud hated that noise. At the first roar of the vacuum, he scooted upstairs and crawled under Susie's bed.

In the bushes Fluffo sat and watched bugs go by. He poked a few with his big paw. Some got squashed. Some got away. He got bored with bugs, so he walked over to the dog's yard next door.

The garage door was open just enough for
him to squeeze in. There were many interesting places here to nose around in.

When Mom finished vacuuming, she told
Susie, "Get Pud and tie him up outside.
I've got all the dog hair off the furniture.

I want to keep it off until our guest gets here."

Susie stuck her head under the bed and waved Pud's leash at him. That meant going for a walk, so he followed her.

Outside she looked for something to tie him to. She decided not to use the lawn chairs. "You're not taking another chair for a walk," she said.

Susie saw the garage door was open a little. She opened it wider. "You can stay here on your rug," she said. "You always like that." She patted his back, pushed him in, and shut the door.

Instantly Pud smelled cat. Orange cat.

"Susie!" Mom yelled out the back door. "Mrs. Amato just called! She's bringing Eddie over!"

Susie felt worried and glad at the same time. Everybody else was really excited.

"What do you think he'll look like?" asked Eric.

"Maybe he'll be a baseball player," said Tim.

"Or a scientist," said Megan, "with brown hair."

"Or a pirate," said Annie, giggling, "with a big, black moustache!"

"No, a dinosaur," said Susie, "with long, blond hair!"

After they stopped laughing, Mom got them to put away a few more things. "Now we're as ready as we'll ever be," she said.

Bong-bong went the doorbell.

Susie's heart went *thud*.

"Do you want to open the door?" asked Dad.

"No, you," she said. She peeked from behind him as he opened it.

There stood a tall man, older than Dad, with some gray in his brown hair. Next to him stood a boy about Susie's age.

"I'm Eddie Shannon," said the man. "And this is my grandson, Matt."

Chapter 8

Susie was amazed. Eddie was somebody's grandfather!

Mrs. Amato came in with them.

"How did you find him?" asked Mom.

"It was easy," said Mrs. Amato. "I grew up in this neighborhood, too. Eddie's older sister was my best friend. We're still friends. I called her and got his phone number."

Eddie looked around. "Whenever I drove past here to show my family my old home, I wished I could come in. This is really a treat."

"We want to show you every room," said Mom.

"Great," said Eddie. "But first I'd like to see what the kids dug up."

He laughed when he saw the rusty old lunch box. "Can you believe it, Matt? I buried this in the backyard so long ago, I don't even remember what I put in it."

Eddie opened the box. "Thirty-five cents was big money when I was little," he said. "I wonder why I wanted to bury so much money. Maybe I thought it was like a pirate treasure."

He unfolded the message. He smiled as he read it. "My spelling wasn't too good in those days. It's much better now."

"How old are you?" asked Megan.

"Fifty-seven," Eddie answered.

"Oh," said all the kids, amazed.

"That seems really old to you," said Eddie, "but not to me."

Susie handed him the baseball card. "This was in there, too," she said.

"Joe DiMaggio!" said Eddie. "My favorite. I had a great baseball card collection. My mother threw them all out after I grew up. My comic books, too. Nobody knew they would ever be collectors' items."

"You can have this one back," said Susie.

"Are you sure?" asked Eddie.

"You're our friend," she said. "You buried the treasure for us to find."

"It's not exactly a treasure," said Eddie, "but it means a lot to me."

"No, it's a real treasure," said Megan.

"I want to tell," said Eric. He pulled the copy of the page from the baseball card book out of his pocket. While he was unfolding it, Annie said, "It's a hundred-dollar one!"

"You're kidding," said Matt.

Eddie looked at the page. "You're not kidding! You deserve a reward for finding this."

"We all helped," said Megan.

"Then you all deserve a reward. And the dog, too. Where is this great dog?"

Out in the garage Pud growled and snarled, but the cat just hissed horribly at him. Fluffo quickly squeezed between a big box and the wall. Now that noisy yapper with the big teeth could not get at him.

Since Pud could not chase the cat out of his garage, he did not want to get any closer to that hissing fur ball. He did not know what to do next.

Fluffo did not know what to do, either. They both sat down. They were stuck there with each other.

Susie opened the garage door. "Come on," she said. "Eddie wants to see you."

Pud really wanted to get out of the garage.

He galloped out past Susie and waited by the back door. She stopped to pull the garage door shut.

A blur of orange fur zoomed out and almost knocked her over.

"Fluffo was in the garage with Pud," Susie told Megan. "Maybe they decided to be friends."

Eddie patted Pud and talked to him. Pud licked Eddie's nose. "He reminds me of my old dog, Dusty," said Eddie. "We weren't supposed to let him upstairs. He got dog hair all over. But my brother Tom and I left our door open at night for him. He sneaked up and slept between our beds."

"Pud sleeps next to my bed," said Susie. "He gets dog hair all over, too." She took Eddie and Matt to see her room.

"This was our room," said Eddie. "We had model airplanes and books and stuff all over. It was always a mess."

Eddie put his arm around Matt. "This house brings back lots of memories. Everywhere I look, I remember my mom and dad and sister and brother so long ago."

Then he laughed. "I just remembered something else. We had a secret hiding place."

He opened the closet and pressed on a floorboard. Nothing happened. He tried another one. "It's here somewhere," he said. He pressed one more. The other end popped up! He showed Matt and Susie the empty space under it.

"Tom and I used to hide things here for fun. Now it's yours, Susie."

Mom and Dad invited Eddie to come back soon with his whole family to show them his old home. Mom took pictures of the kids and Pud with Eddie and Matt and Mrs. Amato.

Susie gave Eddie his lunch box, message,

pencil, and eraser. He gave the pencil and eraser to Matt. He wanted Susie to keep the thirty-five cents.

"When you're fifty-seven," he said, "those old coins might be worth a lot of money. You never know."

For rewards he gave ten dollars to Susie and five dollars each to the other kids. He kneeled down and tucked five dollars in Pud's collar. "Buy something nice for him," he told Susie.

"What do you say?" asked Mom.

They all thanked Eddie. "Thanks so much for the secret hiding place, too," said Susie.

She showed Pud a doggie treat. "Say thank you," she said. "Speak!"

"Woof!" said Pud. He gobbled up the doggie treat.

Matt told his grandfather, "Let's bury a time capsule in my yard."

Dad made Susie put her money in the bank until she decided what to buy. Susie put Pud's five dollars in the secret hiding place for a few days. Then she spent it on a giant box of his favorite doggie treats.

Chapter 9

Susie wanted to bury another time capsule, too.

"Then some kids like us can dig it up a long time from now," she told her friends.

"What'll we use for a treasure?" asked Tim.

"A ten-cent baseball card," said Eric. "When somebody digs it up in a hundred years, it might be a hundred-dollar one."

"Let's all put something in," said Susie. "Everybody bring your stuff over here Saturday morning."

"We can bury it in my yard this time," said Megan.

"No, it's my yard's turn," said Annie.

"We already have a soft, easy hole in my yard," said Susie. "Digging a new one is too hard."

"I'll write the message," decided Megan.

That irked Susie. She wanted to do it.

"No, I want to," said Eric.

"I wanted to do it," said Tim.

Susie sighed. "Then everybody write one."

She asked Mom for something to put the new treasure in. Mom found a big plastic container in the refrigerator. It had some leftover gravy in it.

"Give Pud the gravy," she said. "Then wash this out."

Susie put the gravy in Pud's dish. He lapped it up and looked at her hopefully. "All gone," she said. She used the hose to wash the container.

Susie wanted to put something really good in the treasure. She decided on a tiny stuffed dinosaur. Dad gave her a wallet card with a calendar on it. Mom gave her a picture of everybody with Eddie.

Saturday morning they met at the hole. It was easy to dig this time.

Susie put her stuff in the container. Eric and Tim took scarves out of their pockets. They tied them at the backs of their heads like pirates.

"Yo, ho, ho," said Tim loudly.

"Yo," said Eric. "Now we are ready to put our pirate treasure into the treasure chest."

Eric put in his baseball card. Tim put in a red yo-yo and a sparkling necklace.

Susie clapped her hands. "Jewels for the pirate chest!" she exclaimed.

"It's my mom's old broken necklace," Tim explained. "The yo-yo's broken, too."

Megan put in a plastic dinosaur. "I wrote

my message from Dinosaur Megan," she said. They all laughed.

Annie said, "Everybody knows dinosaurs don't know how to write."

"Maybe the kids who dig this up will think this is the first one that could," said Megan, giggling.

Susie wished she'd thought of that.

Annie put in a pencil with her name on it and a quarter.

Susie squashed everything down to make room for the messages. She put the top on tightly and stuck the container in the hole. They covered it with dirt.

Now their treasure would be buried for a hundred years.

Chapter 10

Early next morning Susie let Pud out in the backyard to go. She watched from the window.

He sniffed around as usual. He stopped at a whiff of that great gravy! He started digging fast.

Before Susie got to him, he dug up the container. He found the smell, but no gravy.

"There wasn't any food in there," said Susie. "What was he digging for?"

"Probably the gravy," said Mom. "Dogs are much better smellers than we are." They found a new container that never had food in it.

Just before Susie buried the new one, Annie came over and took back her quarter.

Next morning when Susie took Pud out, the hole was dug up again. This time the treasure was gone!

She ran around to tell her friends. Megan said "Did anybody know we buried it besides us?" Annie said she did not dig it up to take her pencil back. "I thought about it," she said, "but I didn't do it."

The mystery was solved at Tim's. "My mom found out I buried her necklace. She was really mad. I had to get it back."

"But it was broken," said Susie.

"She was going to get it fixed," said Tim. "I didn't know it had real jewels. I should have asked first."

"Now we don't have any jewels in our treasure," Susie said.

"Yes we do," said Tim. "My mom gave

me a broken earring to put in. She said it's cheap, and she lost the other one anyway." He promised to bring the treasure back as soon as he wrote a new message that said earring and not necklace.

Later that day they buried the treasure again.

That night Susie wished she had her little dinosaur back. Besides, Megan's dinosaur was in there. One was enough.

In the morning she went out to dig up her dinosaur. The treasure was dug up and gone again!

This time it had to be Megan or Eric. Susie decided not to worry about it.

Eric came over later with the container. "I thought I put in a ten-cent baseball card, but I made a mistake," he said. "It was a two-dollar one, so I had to get it back."

Susie took out her dinosaur and put in a little plastic teddy bear. She had another one of those. They pushed the dirt back into the hole.

"No more digging," said Susie.

Annie came around the side of the house. "I need my pencil back," she said.

"You have another one with your name on it," said Susie.

"I lost it," said Annie. They dug again and got the pencil out. Annie put in a blue comb with three teeth broken off.

"Are you sure you won't want this comb back?" asked Susie.

"I'm sure. It isn't even mine. I found it on the sidewalk."

"This is fun," said Eric, throwing dirt at the hole. "Let's keep digging this up and putting more stuff in."

"The stuff we put in keeps getting worse," said Susie. "We're not digging this up anymore."

"Then I'll bury a treasure in my yard,"

said Eric. "I'll dig it up anytime I feel like it. You can come over and help dig it up, too."

"Okay," said Susie. Annie and Eric went over to Eric's.

Pud sat in the yard watching Susie push dirt into the hole. The dirt there smelled like people now. No dog would ever bury a bone there again.

Megan came out of her back door. A blur of orange fur sped by her. Fluffo stopped when he saw Pud. Pud just sat there. Megan picked Fluffo up and scratched his ears.

"See?" said Susie. "I told you they were friends now."

"I'll hold Fluffo, just in case," said Megan. "Are you digging that up again?"

"You want your dinosaur back?" asked Susie.

"No, but if you're digging," said Megan, "I found an old eraser I want to put in there."

Susie burst out laughing and started digging again.